On the Day the Horse Got Out

AUDREY HELEN WEBER

L B
Little, Brown and Company
New York • Boston

On the day the horse got out,

the bells all rang,

the birds flew south,

the spider wove a giant web,

and the roses cried out from their bed:

"WATCH OUT,
WATCH OUT,
the horse is out!"

On the day the horse got out,

the clouds all cried,

the frog had doubts,

the rabbit dug a bit too deep,

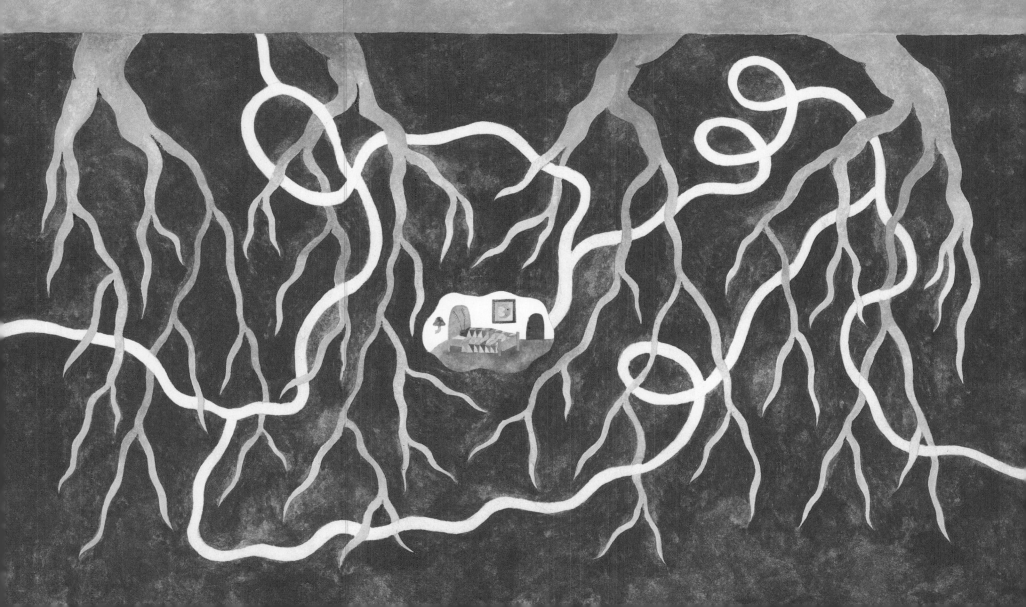

and the beetle cried out in its sleep:

"WATCH OUT, WATCH OUT, *the horse is out!*"

On the day the horse got out,

the eggs all broke,

the ants played house,

the Clouded Skipper lost a wing,

and the eagle cried out to the wind:

"WATCH OUT, WATCH OUT, *the horse is out!*"

On the day the horse got out,

the kids all danced,

the dog was found,

the green fly said, "So long! Goodbye!"

and the comet cried out in the sky:

"Watch out,
watch out,

the horse is out!"